Desert Dan

Also by Elizabeth Coatsworth

THE CAVE
THE NOBLE DOLL
JOCK'S ISLAND
THE HAND OF APOLLO

Desert Dan

BY ELIZABETH COATSWORTH

ILLUSTRATED BY HARPER JOHNSON

The Viking Press

NEW YORK

With this book the author pays tribute to Vassar College
on the occasion of its centennial.

Fic. 1. Animal stories
2. The West

Lithographed in U. S. A. by Halliday Lithograph Corp.

For

Margaret Coatsworth Smith

with a lifetime's

gratitude and love

It was late afternoon, and a touch of coolness was coming across the valley as old Desert Dan made camp by the small spring he had found near the mouth of a canyon. The three burros were already hobbled and grazing nearby; Hector, the bantam rooster, was strutting about underfoot, and now Dan was pegging out Sarah, the goat, near the little covered wagon, where he could keep his eye on her and see that she was safe, for Dan loved Sarah and was careful of her, though she was not much interested in anyone but herself.

It was while Dan was straightening his back, a little slowly these days, that he noticed a jack rabbit, half hidden by a cactus. The animal was paying no attention to the stir about the camp. Something else interested him far more, and he was listening to it with all his might.

Just then a crow went by, flying south and in haste. Another followed.

"Crows usually mean that the coyotes are hunting," Dan said to Sarah the goat, speaking out loud to her as he did to all his household of animals.

But Sarah, as usual, paid no attention to anything that did not concern her, and Hector the little rooster was also aware only of his own affairs.

Now, out of nowhere, buzzards appeared, and without a single flap of their wings circled the spot toward which the crows had flown—the center, too, of the jack rabbit's tense interest. And now a pair of hawks swung into sight to see the fun, whatever it was. Dan glanced at the burros. They, too, were all listening, their big ears pricked forward.

True to his name, Lazy, the gray Mexican burro, soon dropped his head to snatch a bite of greasewood, but Daisy, the white boss burro, never stirred. She held her muzzle high, straining to catch some message along the air. Dan knew that she was worried. The truly excited burro, however, was Crazy, who had been a wild burro in his time. He was trembling, half with fear and half with rage, and moving his hobbled forefeet nervously.

Suddenly the buzzards drifted lower, and at that moment old Dan caught the sound of coyotes closing in on some quarry.

He shook his head sadly, picking Hector up, as much

to comfort himself as to put the little rooster in a place of safety.

"It will be over by now," he said. But he was wrong. Before the words were out of his mouth, one of the crows reappeared, this time flying toward the camp, apparently watching something which moved fast along the ground in Dan's direction. Instantly a new and greater excitement seized the burros. Mexican Lazy stopped feeding, white Daisy began to shuffle forward toward whatever it might be that was coming, and Crazy, braying loudly, hurried off into the chaparral in a series of rocking-horse bounds, getting along surprisingly fast in spite of his hobbles.

Now Daisy was braying too, and, guided by their calls, something burst out of the greasewood. It was a half-grown burro colt, closely pursued by a single coyote. Instantly the grown burros closed in about her, facing the enemy. Even hobbled, their rearing front hoofs could break a coyote's back.

The pursuer, seeing them, slowed to a trot, his tongue hanging far out, so that he seemed to be laughing. His hunting companion, the crow, settled down to await events on a boulder above the spring, looked about, gave a disappointed caw, and flapped away. But the coyote would not so quickly admit defeat. He sat down at a little distance, glancing at Dan with the

bantam held in his arms, at the small covered wagon, at the goat, Sarah, whose cold gray eyes and sharp horns were pointed his way, and lastly at the three furious burros on guard around the colt.

With a quick movement of a paw the intruder pinned down a grasshopper and ate it slowly. Then he rose, stretched, and trotted off without a backward glance.

"Good riddance!" called Dan after him, but there was a touch of admiration in his voice.

When the coyote had disappeared, Dan poked about inside the wagon, poured some powdered milk into a pan, mixed it with water from the spring, filled an empty bottle, found a clean rag for a nipple, and then approached the colt, talking to her quietly.

"There, there," he said. "What a pretty little thing you are with your big baby head and the black stripe down your back! And your coat is still soft as feathers. Shall we call you Nina? Nothing will hurt you here, Baby. What happened to your poor Jenny? Did she get snake-bit, or break a leg? She must have been down or the coyotes wouldn't have got her."

Probably Nina had never seen a man before, but all animals trusted old Dan, and then, too, for thousands of years her ancestors had served men, and perhaps that is why she let Dan come up to her and even stood still while he stroked the gray fluff of her first coat, which she was beginning to shed. Later she let him touch the deep scratches on her flanks, where the coyote must have missed his hold at his first spring. Dan put tar on them.

"Nothing you won't get over, Baby," he promised her. "Hi! Stop that, Crazy!" for Crazy, who never admitted that anyone was his master, had sidled up and tried to give him a nip.

It took Dan a long time to teach Nina to use the bottle, but he was patient, and once she began to taste the milk she drank it down to the last drop, and from that moment became Dan's long-eared shadow.

That evening, while he was heating a pan of baked beans and boiling his coffee over a small fire, he looked up to see shining in the firelight a pair of eyes without visible body. On meeting his glance they silently withdrew, but a few moments later a coyote began his evening song from the top of the same boulder on which the crow had perched earlier.

"Yip yip yip," went the coyote, sounding like half a dozen coyotes. Then followed the long, mournful, and musical howl. Little Nina almost knocked Dan into the fire trying to get closer to him, but the older burros paid no attention. Some sort of truce had been declared, with the coyote and with the desert. The air, which had been so hot all day, was now cool, and so clear that the stars seemed as near as the mountains. And the coyote had trotted through sage and greasewood and desert holly to the camp of its enemies to sing to them.

Dan listened, smiling a little to himself. Bantam Hector drowsed high on the wagon seat. Soon he would be hanging from the wagon top in the strong parrot cage where he spent the nights, safe from all the dangers of the dark. The burros ate with a cropping sound; the goat, Sarah, was half asleep, chewing in her dreams. Only Nina trembled and stamped as she listened.

On and on went the coyote's song. Suddenly two things happened at once. The full moon showed its rim over the mountains across the valley, flooding the desert with light, and the song stopped in mid-quaver. Where the coyote had been sitting, head pointed to the stars, there was now only emptiness.

It was time to go to bed, and Dan staked out Sarah between the wagon wheels and his sleeping bag; he glanced at the burros' hobbles and lifted Hector the rooster into his cage without waking him.

"What about you, Baby?" he asked Nina. "Shall I stake you out with Sarah?" But it didn't seem necessary. "You won't go far from me or the burros, I guess." Once again he fed her from the bottle, and this time she knew at once what to do.

Early in the morning Dan broke camp. It didn't take long. But before he ate his own breakfast he gave Nina her bottle. Then he milked Sarah and tied her to the back of the wagon. He put the little bantam on Daisy's red pack-saddle, where he crowed and flapped his wings, ready to be off. He harnessed the burros with white Daisy in the middle, covered the ashes of his fire with sand, filled the water barrel at the spring, put his sleeping bag and cooking things in the wagon, and, with a last glance to make sure that everything at the camp site was in order, swung into the driver's seat, clucked to Daisy the boss burro, and they were off.

It was a beautiful time of the year to be traveling in the desert. Everywhere there were flowers in great patches, whole pools of pink-lavender sand verbena flowing over the tracks they followed, slopes of poppies blowing in the morning wind, cactus flowers, yellow and fruit-red, and the small yellow blossoms of the greasewood.

It was the season of birds, too. The cactus wrens were building among the prickles, the meadow larks were singing, and the little burrowing owls watched the wagon go by from the sandy round doors of their houses. Several times flights of wild duck passed over-

wriggling off into the shelter of a greasewood bush, the white skull of a steer, half-buried in sand.

He saw a jet plane far above him, moving almost without sound. Once their track crossed a highway, and Dan pulled Daisy up while a solitary car rushed by. Once he stopped to feed Nina, and several times he found rare plants, which he dug up and put into some of the empty cans stored in the body of the wagon.

At a deserted shack close to the foot of a cliff he stopped for his own lunch, and there again Nina was fed. Afterward she followed close at Dan's heels as he wandered about, picking up a few old bottles and tumblers which had been thrown on the trash pile long ago and had turned lavender in the glare of the sun. These, too, Dan took back to the wagon and stowed away in a carton, wrapped in newspaper. Nearby, a little stream came out of the canyon only to lose itself in the sand. Dan, followed by Nina, climbed along its course a short way up into the mountains and came back with several moss-agate pebbles in his baggy pockets.

"You bring good luck, Baby," he told her, patting her little white muzzle, "and you're a good rock climber, too. Your Jenny brought you up well."

Nina turned her ears to listen to his voice. Like all the other animals, she liked to hear old Dan talk. As they were ready to drive off, Dan saw a road-runner,

head, going north, having spent the night in some salt-rimmed pool among the rushes.

For a while Nina ran round and round the wagon with rolling eyes, fearful of losing Dan. But Dan kept speaking to her and soon she grew quieter, and at last settled down to trot along beside Mexican Lazy, who was half asleep in the traces, his head low and his long ears wagging.

It was growing hotter and everything drowsed. Hector the rooster was lulled almost into sleep by white Daisy's steady shuffle, Crazy dreamed of the herd of wild burros he had once run with, Lazy remembered his first Mexican master, and Sarah the goat pulled back on her halter with half-shut eyes.

Only old Dan was wide awake. In his lined brown face his eyes were as deep blue as robins' eggs in a nest. He sat motionless on the seat of the wagon, the reins which led to Daisy's bit loose in one hand. Looking from side to side, he saw everything: the humming-bird on her nest, the chuckwalla with its striped tail

that strange-looking bird, and waited until it had crossed the track ahead of them, perhaps off to fight with a rattlesnake.

At the first slap of the reins the leader, Daisy, started up, and the others moved with her. Even Crazy knew that Daisy was boss burro. When she went on, the other burros went on. When she stopped, they stopped. If she turned, they turned, and the wagon with them, and Sarah the goat, plodding on behind, and Nina, trotting now on one side, now on the other. Seven or eight miles a day Dan counted on traveling, but sometimes he camped earlier if he found fresh water, and now and then they went ten or twelve miles to reach a spring. Water was what counted. All the wagon tracks, all the trails of mice and rabbits, of coyotes and deer, ultimately led to water.

During the first day they saw no coyotes or even crows, which keep an eye on the coyotes to see if they have found anything to eat, as the coyotes keep an eye on the crows for the same reason. But that evening their campfire was again serenaded for an hour.

Nina would not, or could not, drink her milk while the coyote was near. She stamped and shivered, shivered and stamped, until Dan stopped what he was doing to lay an arm about her fuzzy neck and quiet her. Even then she could not really relax until the unwelcome visitor was gone.

Two evenings later they had a visitor of another sort. Dan had made camp and was paring potatoes with all the burros crowding about him for their share of the peels, when suddenly Crazy wheeled into action with a loud warning bray. Dan looked up to see a young man walking toward them. The stranger easily side-stepped Crazy, Dan rose to meet him, and they shook hands.

The young man was dark and quiet, with a broad face and black eyes. He was dressed in jeans and a blue shirt, carried a gun on his shoulder, and wore moccasins. His hair was rather long, and he had tied a red bandana around his head instead of wearing

a hat. On one shoulder he carried a bumpy game bag.

"They call me Desert Dan," said Dan as they shook hands.

The other nodded. "I knew who you were. I saw you once at Hot Springs when I was a kid. I'm a Piute. My name's Pete."

"Glad to see you, Pete. I'm just getting supper. Hope you'll join me."

Pete nodded and dropped down on his heels beside the fire. Without speaking he drew out a dead rabbit from the bag, skinned it, and spitted it on a green stick which he held above the fire, while Dan got out the extra cup, plate, spoon, fork, and knife he kept for company, as well as a can of tomatoes and a can of peaches.

With the coffee, it was a desert feast.

They began the meal still in silence, Nina's head almost resting on Dan's shoulder.

Before they were halfway through, the coyote commenced its evening song. Nina flung up her head, but almost at once the singing broke off and the animal was gone.

Pete patted the gun beside him.

"Coyotes know. He saw I had my gun with me. He doesn't like its bark."

Pete did not really smile but there was a smile in his eyes.

"Coyotes kill her mother?" he added, making a

gesture of his head toward Nina. He had noticed her excitement, as he noticed everything.

"Yes. Two or three days ago. She remembers."

"Sure. She'll always remember. She'll always hate coyotes."

Dan nodded and silence again fell until the meal was finished. When Pete came back from washing the dishes besides the spring, he asked, "Had any luck finding gold?"

Dan gave a short laugh. "Anyone with a burro, folks think is hunting for gold. I'm not interested. I've seen too many men kill themselves that way."

The Indian didn't look at him. "Everyone who comes to the desert is hunting for something," he said.

"Yes," agreed Dan, leaning back against a wheel of the cart, while he took out his old pipe and slowly

lighted it. "I hunt for a lot of things. All sorts. I hunt for rare plants, and the seeds of flowers. There's one kind of violet so rare I get fifty cents a seed for it. I've found moonstones—that was two years back—and queer twisted-looking rocks for people's gardens. I pick up desert glass, and old juniper branches, all sorts of things. But never gold, silver, or uranium. I've no use for that stuff."

"What do you think of this?" The young man reached into the game bag and brought up a rounded piece of pottery, which had once been part of a jar. But there was something unusual about this piece of clay. It glistened and glittered with bright specks.

Pete handed it to Desert Dan and the old man turned it about to the light, looked at it briefly, and handed it back. "I don't know much about it," he said after a while. "But I'd agree with you."

"That it's gold?"

"Looks like it to me."

They were silent for some time. Perhaps Pete thought the other man would ask questions, but Dan didn't. In the end it was Pete who spoke.

"My mother used that jar to hold water. I've seen it all my life and never thought about it. But a while ago it got broken and then I looked at it. I asked her where the earth came from she had used to make it.

It was so long ago, she said, that she couldn't remember."

"So now you're hunting for the place."

"Yes. For rabbits, too. And a deer if I can get one."

"If I ever come on clay like that I'll let you know."

Pete gave Dan a quick look. "You mean it. People said you were a good man. I see now they were right."

"I told you. I don't monkey with gold, silver, or uranium. I made that rule a long time ago. I take a good deal of pleasure moseying about deserts. I never yet saw a prospector who took pleasure in anything but in getting rich."

Pete dropped the subject. "Know the country ahead?" he asked.

"Never been there. But I got a map," said Dan.

"Don't trust the map too much. A spring that's all right one year may not be there the next. It's dry country and this has been a dry year. Be careful."

"Thank you. I'll be careful."

That night Pete slept beside Dan's fire. As the flames died down, leaving the glow of coals like an eye, the coyote began singing again, but farther off. Nina crowded up to Dan, waking him. Probably Pete had not been asleep, for he said out of the darkness, "That coyote's sure after something. I'd be careful if I was that burro colt. The fellow out there thinks you

stole her from him and he means to have his dinner yet."

Pete must have reached toward his gun, for all at once the song broke off and the coyote vanished.

That morning the two men were up well before dawn. Pete built the fire while Dan fed Nina, milked Sarah, and made the coffee and flapjacks. They ate in comfortable silence, and then smoked together, Dan puffing at his pipe, Pete at a cigarette. It seemed almost as if they were unwilling to go their separate ways just yet. The mingled smoke drifted above their heads in the quiet air like the smoke of some long-ago peace pipe.

At last Pete sighed and got to his feet, pulled the

game bag back on his shoulder, and picked up the gun. "I have thought of the words you spoke last night," he said, "and you are wise. My mother, too, I think, did not wish me to look for the clay from which she had made the pot."

He gave the slightest of glances toward the ground, and Dan saw that the precious shard was lying among the ashes of their fire.

Then Pete reached out his thin brown hand toward Dan's outstretched hand. His last words were a warning. "Remember, too," Pete said, "what I told you about the springs in the country ahead of you. And be careful. Be very careful."

So they parted, the Piute traveling toward the north, and Dan and his family of animals again taking up the road that wavered southward.

It was a more than usually hot day and everyone suffered. The three burros went slowly, heads hanging, and Sarah dragged at her rope at the tail of the cart. Hector sat not on Daisy's saddle but on the seat beside Dan in the shade of the awning, beak open and wings spread for a little coolness, and Dan kept wiping the sweat out of his blue eyes. Little Nina followed at Sarah's heels, sometimes almost out of sight of the cart. Then she would break into a stumbling trot to catch up again.

As the shadows of the mountains began to lengthen and the evening coolness came into the air, everyone's courage rose.

"Won't be long now," Dan said to his animals, folding up the map. "Lost Spring can't be over a mile off. Maybe less."

But when they came to Lost Spring there was nothing but dried mud. The coyotes had been digging there, but they had found no water. The dry camp Dan made that night was uncomfortable for everyone. Hector had a saucer of water from the small barrel at the back of the wagon. Sarah, the goat, had a good drink, Nina her bottle, and Lazy, Daisy, and Crazy had something. But for them it had to be short rations. A sense of uneasiness hung over the little gathering. That night there was no coyote serenade, but the desert seemed un-

friendly. The great stars were like watchful eyes, waiting as the hawks and buzzards and crows had waited, hanging over the place where Nina's Jenny went down. There were rustlings in the mesquite, and once, not far off, something gave a little shriek.

That night even Crazy stayed close to camp, too tired and thirsty to care much for food, and old Dan slept but little.

Ought he to turn back?

But according to the map there was another spring only seven miles on—New Hope Spring. It was the name that decided Dan. Someone had come there

once, feeling as he and the animals felt now, and the water they found had given them new hope.

Early the next morning, Dan gave each of the burros and Sarah a swallow from what was left in the cask. Nina had her bottle of milk and the bantam Hector had his saucer. Everyone was eager for the road. Somewhere ahead water must be waiting, and they wanted to get to it.

But after the first mile or two their courage drooped. A wind had come up. The sand was blowing. It was like a yellow fog, wrapping the mountains from sight. The sky was no longer blue overhead. It was pale and low and dirty-looking. Each mesquite bush and cactus seemed like a creature crouching beside the road, ready to spring, and the ruts appeared and disappeared like a mirage before the white bobbing muzzles of the burros. The sand blew into their eyes. They breathed it. It gritted between their teeth and sifted into Dan's clothing at every crack. Only Hector could droop on his perch in the parrot cage, his eyes closed, his wings outspread, and doze away the awful hours. The rest must plod on, even Dan, who often walked to lighten the load for the three burros.

He talked to Nina, encouraging her.

"Keep going, Baby, you can't weaken now. That coyote's not going to get you. We'll fool him yet."

And, cheered by his hand on her shoulder, his voice in her ear, little Nina braced forward into the hot wind, shut her eyes, and went on with the others.

Several times they stopped to rest with their backs to the blowing sand, but Dan didn't dare to stop long for fear that they would never get started again. Once he milked Sarah hastily and shared the milk with Nina. There was no water left. In the middle of the afternoon the wind began to go down, and the burros traveled a little faster, the sand clotted in their wet eyelashes. Then Lazy took to stopping. Dan tried to coax him along, but when all else failed he beat him hard with the ends of the reins, forcing himself to yell at the exhausted beast, while Daisy, her white hide yellow with sweat and dust, pulled at his side, hauling him along, though the added effort was telling on her fast. Crazy, ears back, kept up with Daisy. He was mean, but he had plenty of courage, and so, it seemed, did Nina, little as she was. In some ways, next to Hector, Sarah the goat had the best of it. She was partly protected from the sand by the wagon, and when she was exhausted she could drag back on her halter and be pulled along by the burros. But even she was nearly at the end of her strength when, about four o'clock in the afternoon, the burro wagon struggled in to New Hope Spring.

New Hope may once have been a new hope for someone, but for old Dan and his creatures it was black despair. Again they found nothing but dried mud, and scratches which had not reached water. It was like Lost Spring all over again, but this time Dan had no emergency rations in the cart.

They could not go back. The burros would not last two days, nor would Dan, even with Sarah and, for a little while, Sarah's milk. Dan knew what would happen. He wasn't called Desert Dan for nothing. He had traveled the desert for many years, and more than once in his time he had come upon skeletons of men and pack animals.

But at least the burros should have their chance. Talking to them quietly, patting their sweated coats, he unharnessed them, Lazy first, then Daisy, who rubbed her head against his arm, and Crazy, who made a last half-hearted attempt to bite him. Then he took the little rooster Hector in his arms and wound Sarah's rope around his left hand. Nina was close beside him. The wind had died down at last. The pale valley lay all about them, and now the range of black, bare mountains showed in the west, rising sternly above their shadows.

It was Crazy who first realized that he was free, with no rope on his halter, no hobbles on his legs. He

threw up his crazy head, breathed deeply, and started shuffling off into the desert. White Daisy followed him, and Old Dan followed her, Sarah dragging a little. Lazy, finding himself deserted, brought up the rear, often falling behind.

Slowly, uncertainly, the procession staggered on, led always by Crazy, but Daisy was still boss burro. It was she who brayed and stopped when old Dan with Nina and Sarah and Hector dropped too far behind. At first Crazy went on without waiting, but in the end Daisy's angry brays pulled him to an unwilling halt, until the stragglers were ready to go on. She stood

between the guide, Crazy, and old Dan and the rest of the animals, who followed as best they could. Once she came back to push with her white muzzle at dragging Sarah. Perhaps she threatened her—Sarah went better afterward. She touched nostrils with Nina and seemed to breathe courage into her. She looked at Dan as though to say, "It will be all right yet, old man." She sent a heartening call to Lazy, out of sight behind the others, and then went on, and somewhere ahead the impatient Crazy snorted and started off again.

As it grew dark, Daisy kept closer to the others.

Old Dan was walking more and more slowly. But now Daisy no longer tried to call Crazy back. She seemed not to care where he went, for she herself moved without her earlier hesitation. Some message had reached Lazy. He appeared from the rear and hurried off in Crazy's track. Of the working burros, only Daisy stayed behind with her master, and now Nina was pricking up her long ears, and the goat was hurrying ahead, unconsciously helping Dan as she pulled at her rope, though helping anyone was never part of her plan. Even Hector, under Dan's arms, began to stir and cluck.

A loud bray ahead rang across the desert and Daisy

answered it, Lazy took it up, and Nina joined in. They were sending the news up and down the line. Sarah bleated. She understood. Hector clucked again and louder and old Dan mumbled, "They've found water."

Ten minutes later they were all at the spring, drinking the muddy contents as if it were the finest thing in the world. Dan and the burros knew better than to drink too much at a time. As for Sarah, Dan pulled her away after a few long swallows. "That will do, that will do," he warned her, and she stared at him angrily from her pale eyes.

It was a wonderful night. The stars had lost their hungry look, and the coolness came down the canyons like a river. Dan put his back against a stone and slept and woke up and slept again with little Hector picketed close by. In the first dawn he opened his eyes to see a coyote drinking downwind on the other side of the water hole. None of the burros scented him and the coyote drank as if he were all alone, unhurriedly. Then he stared at Dan, looking straight into his face, sat down to scratch an ear, and trotted off. In a moment the black tip of his tail had disappeared.

Very early, Dan led his cavalcade back to get the wagon, and by mid-morning they were again camping at the spring, taking a day's rest before going on. By daylight Dan could see how many trails from every direction led to the water, the trails of mice and pack rats, of rabbits and badgers and coyotes, and the little trails of the crested quail. Most interesting to him was a wagon track which showed recent tire marks. Near it someone had painted on a rock "Hallelujah Mine, five miles," with a pointing arrow.

"I guess that's a kind of invitation," said old Dan to his family. "But we'll rest up a bit and tomorrow we'll go calling."

During the first night at the spring it had been too cold for him to get much sleep without his blankets, but now he dozed in the shade of a mesquite bush and woke up much refreshed. Hector was restless in his cage under the hot wagon-cover and Dan took him out and let him amuse himself hunting for insects along the edge of the water hole. Suddenly, out of what had seemed clear air, a hawk plummeted down toward the bantam. Before Dan could move, Hector wrenched himself free and, jumping high in the air, struck with

his spurs at the low-hovering enemy. A shout from Dan sent the intruder soaring away, while the little rooster clapped his wings and crowed in triumph.

That afternoon, when the cooler air began to flow again, Dan went off to see what he could see: a rare

plant, a bright stone, anything that people might like. As usual, Nina went with him, and it was her curiosity that found the entrance to the cave.

At first it seemed a small cave, its opening hidden behind mesquite bushes. When Nina disappeared into it, Dan had to follow on his hands and knees, but Nina entered as if it had been made for her. Inside, the ceiling rose and Dan, too, could stand upright, but it was some time before he found the old Indian storage basket on a natural shelf far back in the shadows. It was about two feet high and was decorated with zigzag patterns of brown bark woven along its curving sides. Inside, there lay a powdery remnant of the roots and nuts that long-dead Indians had left there, intending to return, but for some reason never coming back.

Dan brought it to the light, touching it with careful hands. As Nina crowded too close, he flapped his bandana at her and she pretended to shy away in terror.

It took Dan a long time to decide how to pack the basket in the burro wagon. At last he hung it in a net of ropes from the top beside Hector's cage.

"That's good enough for a museum," old Dan said, as he brought Nina a rewarding bottle of milk. "But I may want to keep it for myself. It's the finest thing I ever found on the desert. Excuse me, Baby, *you* found it."

That day was a holiday for everyone, and, leaving Hector safe in his cage, Dan and Nina went off again exploring. They found nothing, and weren't away long, but when they came back a coyote jumped out of the tail of the wagon with a piece of dried meat in his mouth. Quick as a wink, Dan picked up a stone and threw it at the robber. It hit the coyote in the ribs, the beast dropped the meat, and before he could snatch it up again a crow grabbed it and flew heavily away. The coyote looked after the crow, surprised and furious at the theft.

Dan couldn't help laughing. "But I'm kind of sorry I threw that stone," he apologized to the retreating coyote. "After all, you have to live, and I suppose you're hungry most of the time."

By the next day, everyone was rested and ready to go on, and the wagon started off for Hallelujah Mine. There was nothing very interesting along the way, except that on some of the rocks there were Indian pictographs, mostly of deer, with heads all pointed toward the spring.

"I'll bet those pictographs are water signs," said Dan. "Pity we didn't have any on our side of the valley. But, Crazy, you did just as well. Though much good that would have done, if Daisy hadn't been there to take care of us."

In the middle of the afternoon the wagon, jogging along slowly, came to a gulch where two cabins stood in a grove of cottonwoods. Above them on the steep slope of the mountain was the opening of a mine which had been recently worked, like a large gopher hole, with the earth still fresh at the entrance.

As the burros forded the trickle of a stream below the cabins, they saw that on the rough steps of the one nearer the water a yellow dog was lying, watching them. Dan pulled up the burros, always willing to stop, swung down from the wagon seat, and walked toward

the cabin with Nina close behind. The dog got up,
growling but at the same time wagging her yellow
brush of a tail. She wanted to be friendly, but she was
on guard, although the shack was empty. The door
was hanging open and a heap of old bottles and papers
and recently thrown away clothes lay about on the
ground. One of the windows was broken, and already
birds were flying in and out as if they owned the place.

Dan shouted, "Anyone home?" and his voice echoed against the mountain sides. "Anyone home?"

The dog bristled and stood her ground, and the birds flew out noisily. No one answered from the house, but a thickset woman in a faded cotton dress appeared at the door of the next cabin and stared down at Dan and his covered wagon.

"I suppose you're the one they call Desert Dan," she said without greeting, in a voice which didn't seem to have been much used lately. She came out on the steps

and her movement away from the door brought to light two small children hiding close behind her skirts.

"Yes, ma'am," said Dan, "that's what they call me. If you don't mind my asking, who are you? This is one road I've never followed."

The woman grew more friendly. Really, she had been friendly from the first, but she had forgotten how people act when they see a stranger. Once she began to talk, she could hardly stop. She told him that her name was Mrs. Chuck Davis and that the mine was called the Hallelujah and this child was Chad and the smaller one was Annabel, and her husband was working the mine alone now and would soon be back for his grub. His partner, Lonnie Sims, if you could call him a partner, went off last week, the pay dirt was

running so low, but her husband meant to stick it out a while longer. That dog, Chino—she wasn't what you could rightly call a dog. She was half coyote, and when the coyotes were around she'd go off and run with them, maybe a week at a time. Sometimes they came calling for her like a lot of boys stopping at another boy's house to get him to go off with them, and off she'd go, though she always got an awful walloping from Lonnie when she came back. She'd been gone when Lonnie decided to throw in his hand. That's why he left without her. Now she seemed to feel bad, if a dog that was half coyote *could* feel bad. She seemed afraid he'd come back and find her gone again. She wouldn't leave that step. It didn't much matter about a critter like that, but you couldn't see a dog die before your eyes even if she *was* half coyote. So she, Mrs. Chuck, had gone over now and then with some scraps. Chuck, her husband, said she was a fool to do it.

"It's what any kind woman would do," said Dan, smiling at Mrs. Davis, as he invited her to bring the children to watch him make camp.

They all three came, Mrs. Chuck carrying a big loaf of freshly baked bread. Dan soon had the children talking like sparrows in the ivy. They weren't used to people, but Dan wasn't like other people. He put Chad

on Daisy's back and Annabel on Lazy's and led them
for a ride. (But he warned them to keep away from
Crazy. "Most of the time," he told them, "he's only
pretending to be bad-tempered, but sometimes he pre-
tends too hard, and it hurts.")

Then he milked the goat, and gave them all some
fresh milk. The bubbles got into the children's noses,
which made them laugh, and Mrs. Chuck kept telling
everyone about the cow her father had given her when
she was a girl back in Iowa.

The children wanted to pat Hector's feathers and
he let them, but soon he showed he'd rather hunt for
ants than be petted any more. If course it was Nina

they all were most interested in, and Nina liked nothing better than to be patted and scratched behind the ears, in the way Dan showed the children, while Mrs. Chuck looked on, happy to see the young ones having such a good time.

"It's lonely for them," she said. "We don't see a new

face for months on end. But Chuck's a good husband. I knew he was a miner when I married him."

It wasn't long afterward that Chuck appeared, a thin, rather stooped-over man with a week's beard and kind eyes. Like the Indian, he tried to find out if Dan was looking for gold.

"No," Dan said, whittling away at the toy boats he was making for Chad and Annabel. "I'm not. I'm just what some people call a desert rat. Years ago I once crossed the desert with my wife and I never forgot about it. We bought a little fruit ranch in the valley. I liked it, but all the time I was remembering the desert. Then my wife died. We didn't have any family, so there was nothing to hold me. Now my home's that little covered wagon and my family all have four legs —except the bantam, Hector, of course. They're a good family and I think I'm about as fond of them as other men are of theirs."

"And they're just as fond of you!" said Mrs. Chuck, warmly.

Dan asked the Davises to stay for supper, and after making some excuses they did. Mrs. Chuck brought down pickles and jam she'd made from cactus pears, and they all had a good time with Nina's white nose stuck between Chad and Annabel for the bread crusts they kept feeding her.

Chuck said, looking at the sky, that a storm was blowing up, and at last they all went home, turning around again and again to call and wave. When they were gone, old Dan climbed the slope once more to the empty shack with some scraps for the dog on lonely guard by the door.

"Look here, Chino," he told her when she had finished wolfing down the food, "Chuck says the mine's about played out. Like as not the Davises will leave all of a sudden, too, just like Lonnie. And *then* what will you do? Stay here and starve? You've got me worried. I don't know as I need a dog that's half coyote, but if you'd like to come along, maybe we'll make out together. At least we can try."

But Chino would not make friends, let alone come along. She wouldn't even let him touch her, but showed her teeth and pulled back. Yet all the time she kept whimpering under her breath.

At last Dan gave up.

"Maybe you'll feel different when you've had time to think it over," he told her. "I'll be along in the morning. Don't be silly, Chino. You're doing yourself no good here."

When he turned, he was surprised to find that for once Nina wasn't right behind him. She stood some way off, looking frightened and at the same time mean, ready to rear and strike out with her small front hoofs.

Dan whistled.

"Afraid of dogs?" he asked her, "or only of dogs that are half coyote?"

Nina followed him back to the camp, turning her head to make sure that Chino wasn't behind them. Even by the fire among the other animals, it was a long time before she stopped being on the lookout, and that evening she kept closer than ever to Dan's side.

"What's scared you?" Dan asked. "That Chino wouldn't hurt you. Or is it the thunder and lightning?"

The storm that Chuck had felt in the air was now gathering in the mountaintops. At briefer and briefer intervals, lightning shattered the darkness, the thunder seemed to be knocking the granite peaks together, and the leaves of the cottonwoods were shaking back and forth, making a loud whispering.

Old Dan went all around his camp, looking for signs that the water had ever reached so far up, but there were none. He hobbled the burros with extra care, tied Sarah to a wagon wheel, put Hector early to bed, and laid out his own sleeping bag in the body of the wagon. But before he crawled in to sleep, or to try to sleep, he found a newspaper clipping in an old coffee tin where he kept such things, and read it in the last light of day.

Nina was at his shoulder, so he read it aloud to her.

"This here's a Pima Indian storm song," he told her. "I found it in a Bakersfield paper once and I always take it out when a big how-de-do like this is blowing up. Makes me enjoy it more, somehow. Now listen and stop teasing for crusts. They're all gone." And he read slowly, chanting the words.

> "Wind, now commence to sing;
> Wind, now commence to sing.
> The land stretches before me,
> Before me stretches away.

> "Wind's house now is thundering;
> Wind's house now is thundering.
> I go roaring o'er the land,
> The land covered with thunder.

> "Over the windy mountains,
> Over the windy mountains,
> Came the many-leggèd wind;
> The wind came running hither.

> "The Black Snake Wind came to me;
> The Black Snake Wind came to me;
> Came and wrapped itself about,
> Came here running with its song."

"See what they mean? The way that wind kind of wraps round your legs like a snake? Well, we'd better get some sleep."

But that night there was not much sleep for anyone. The storm raged like a crazy thing, back in the mountains, and to make it worse the coyotes were yapping and somewhere a mountain lion began crying in a high shriek, again and again repeated. Then it started to rain in torrents. The voices of the trees were drowned out now in the roar of the water racing down the canyon. What had been a trickle in the afternoon, by midnight was a river, sweeping all before it.

Dan got up and wandered about, wet and uneasy. A lamp had been lighted in the Davis cabin. Their house was well out of reach of any flash flood, but it seemed to Dan that water was washing about the foundations of the empty shack nearer the stream. The lightning came down in sheets, showing the burros huddled together, looking miserable, and flaring on canyon walls and cabins.

In such a light Dan saw a fifteen-foot high wave roaring down the channel. Before his eyes, Lonnie's former cabin toppled over on its side and began its slow twirling journey down the flood.

"Chino!" he shouted. "Chino!"

But no Chino came to his call.

Dan began scrambling down the bank to the edge of the water. A cottonwood had toppled into it, most of its roots undermined by the current, but some roots were still holding, so that the trunk and branches formed a breakwater, already wedged with debris. Along this Dan made his way quickly, partly by feel and partly in the flares of lightning. From here he was barely in time to reach out and catch Chino as she was borne by, half drowned but still struggling. She was too heavy for him to lift, but he worked her slowly back toward the bank, his fingers sunk into the scruff of her neck. At last she felt earth under her

feet and clawed herself to the land, too weak to shake the water out of her coat. Dan, too, was so exhausted that he threw himself flat on the earth beside her, and lay there soaked through and gasping for breath.

But suddenly, above the sound of the river and the rain and his own panting, he heard the charging patter of hoofs. It was Nina, and Nina ready for war, a wet, rearing Nina, a Nina with ears laid back, as Dan saw in a torch of living fire while he dragged himself to his feet to drive her away. But Nina was beside herself with rage. She tried to circle out of his reach, to run in under his outstretched arm, by any means to get at that bundle of wet fur which to her meant coyote and killer.

The lightning crackled, the thunder echoed between the canyon walls. Below them the roots of the cottonwood tree were finally loosened from their hold, and down the river it went, like a leafy island. And still Dan and Nina circled about Chino, until at last the dog got to her feet and Nina knew that her chance for revenge was over.

Back to the camp they trailed, Dan leading, Chino close at his heels, and Nina following far in the rear. That was the order in which they went thereafter, and no coaxing or scolding from Dan could change it. By morning the storm was over and the sun was bright in hanging raindrops. Chuck Davis came down to camp to borrow some sugar and to tell how one of the cabin windows had blown open during the night and the children's bed had been soaked through.

Dan gave him a cup of hot coffee and went back with him to the cabin. This time Chad and little Annabel ran out to meet him and brought him home, each swinging on a hand.

Mrs. Chuck made a great fuss over him. "I'm tickled pink to see you're all right, and I can tell by your face no harm's come to your family, either. Worried all night about you. Oh no, we're fine, thank you. The children just crawled into a dry quilt and slept on the floor. See you have that dog of Lonnie's with you now. Hope she won't do anything she oughtn't. Don't say I didn't warn you she was half coyote."

Getting off that morning was a slow business, for both the children tried to help Dan pack and harness up, and he let them. Another thing that delayed him was trying to make Nina accept Chino as a new member of the family.

"She won't hurt you, Baby," he promised. "See, she wants to make friends," and indeed Chino made every effort, but Nina would have none of her. At last Dan was ready to break camp and they were off with the yellow dog, still exhausted from her ordeal,

sitting beside him on the driver's seat, and Hector
crowing from his perch once more on Daisy's pack
saddle, and the children running beside them, and
Mrs. Chuck waving a dishcloth from the cabin door,
and Chuck waving a lonely bandana from the mine
opening.

It was a nice going off, but a little sad, too. As for

poor Nina, she followed the wagon at Sarah's heels instead of trotting beside the other burros as usual.

That night not one but two or three coyotes sang outside the camp. Chino pricked up her ears, but stayed close by the fire.

"You can go with them if you want to," Dan told her, but she only wagged her yellow brush and stared at him in the firelight.

Again Nina was too upset to finish her bottle of milk, and of her own accord she still wouldn't come within twenty feet of Chino. Dan tied her to the wagon wheel for the night.

"I'm afraid by the way you're hanging off in the shadows, the coyotes may get you yet," he said, patting her, but, though she rubbed her head against his chest, the weight on her heart was not lightened.

For the next few days their way led along a mesa

among bush lupins with blue spires like the blue glass in church windows. Chino, rested now, trotted behind the wagon beside Sarah, or ranged in the chaparral, chasing rabbits. But she was never gone long. Always she came back, and always Nina avoided her. Now it was Chino who helped Dan in his daily search for things to take back in the cart. If she found no storage basket in a cave, one day she did find the skull of a mountain sheep with the great curl of its horns still white and perfect. Dan was almost as pleased as he had been with Nina's basket. He sat down on his heels to study it. The ram must have been young, for the tips of its horns had not yet been broken by digging for edible roots among the rocks.

Then he stood up and hefted it. It was heavy.

"I bet that weighs thirty pounds," he said to Chino, but then he realized that Chino, who had been there only a moment before, was gone.

"I hope she won't scare Nina," he thought, immediately glancing along the back trail for the little burro, who had been following well behind. But Nina, too, had disappeared. He whistled, but neither dog nor burro colt came in sight.

A crow flew by overhead. And then its mate followed. That might mean much or nothing, but just then he saw the first buzzard circling.

Dan dropped the bighorn's skull and started running toward the spot above which the buzzard hovered. He seemed to be moving in a nightmare, once more reliving the death of Nina's mother. As before, curiosity had brought even the little hawks.

And now, through his panting, Dan heard the snarl and yap of fighting coyotes. Poor little Nina, with her muzzle like a white teacup and the white saucers around her eyes! Dan guessed all too well what had happened. Finding her so far away from him, a coyote had got between them and quietly driven her off to a safe spot where the rest of the pack could set on her undisturbed.

It must be all over by now.

But it wasn't. The sounds of fighting were still going on. Neither the buzzard nor the crows had settled down to the earth. And so old Dan kept running.

It was then, when he was almost out of his last breath, and his heart seemed the largest thing in his old body, that Nina appeared, tearing along at full speed, her big head out straight and her little hoofs flying. This time, too, there was a coyote running at her heels, and once more there was blood on Nina's soft coat, but now there was more blood on the coyote. Never pausing, both animals tore up to Dan, nearly knocking him down in their excitement and joy.

"Why—why—" stammered old Dan. "If Chino hasn't brought Baby home, safe and sound! What a fight you two must have made of it! There were at least three coyotes trying to finish her."

He hugged them, he patted them, he made much

of them, and they made much of him and of each other. Nina bent her muzzle down to Chino, and Chino lapped it and jumped up against her shoulder, and this time Nina never flinched, but curved her woolly neck down to meet the friend who had saved her.

"I never was gladder of anything in my whole life," said Desert Dan. "To think that you're both back safe and back together! Now someday Crazy can go live with the wild burros the way he wants to, and Baby will take his place, and we'll have good times together, with Chino to guard us all."

And so, in the greatest content, the three walked back to camp, and that night there was no evening song, for the leader of the coyotes must have given up all hope of ever getting Nina, now, and, being an animal with a great deal of common sense, he must have trotted off to take himself and his hunting elsewhere.